THE RAVEN
ON THE
ROSE BUSH

Roger Dylan Turner

To order additional copies of this book, contact:
Xlibris
844-714-8691
www.Xlibris.com
Orders@Xlibris.com

ISBN: Softcover   978-1-6698-3583-7
          EBook   978-1-6698-3582-0

Print information available on the last page

Rev. date: 07/05/2022

The Raven on the Rosebush

CHAPTER 1

Our story begins in a little old town, and in this little old town, there stood a little old house, and in this little old house, there lived a little old man and two big old pets. The man was a college historian and fitted the type of a reclusive scholar well. But for all their biographies and speeches, many books in that field are lifeless and fail to speak to the soul. While with peers or students, he could discuss everything, from great battles to great inventions, but his conversation turned awkward when it came to common articles.

So seeking a friendship that would not require many words, the professor went to the pound to examine its unwilling residents. Among them, he found a haggard dog and an equally disfigured cat. Though he never learned their respective stories, it was clear that hunger, cold, and hopelessness had worn them to near-death. His studies of our species' growth served to heighten his own humanity, and with conscience pricked, he decided to resurrect these miserable creatures.

As soon as they were home, the professor proceeded to pamper them with passion. His meals were their meals, and his bed was their bed. The next day, he purchased rhinestone collars with bronze name tags, along with pads and litter, and a plethora of playthings. His was a lap of luxury, on which he petted his prized possessions frequently so as to nearly strip them. Though they did not become bald, the dog and cat did become puffed, with pride as much as fat.

A wise ruler once wrote, "The righteous one takes care of his domestic animals," but as one might expect, when such treatment becomes excessive, the appreciation of the receivers gradually dwindles. Their daily schedules were occupied by four burdens: meals, rest, massages, and war. This last ritual will be explained in a moment. But as for their caretaker, his time was not so sweetly spent. Large pets are often the result of a large grocery bill, and though their hurried and constant eating was initially caused by their long deprivation of decent meals, in time, they began to gorge themselves for the grotesque pleasure of gluttony. He had made several attempts to enforce a diet, but each time, it was broken by whining and feigned weariness. Their sizes, while obviously hurting personal health, also had adverse effects on their "master."

heir position in bed, perhaps more than anything else, illustrated the reversal of mastership. At first, and in keeping with the words of an ancient poet, the animals were put "under" the professor's feet, with the dog and cat lying against the left and right soles respectively. In time, they rose to the knees, then hips, until they reached the pillow and started resting their chins on its edges. At first, the professor found this somewhat endearing, even flattering, but then came the night that he heard an awful scrapping, and on coming out of his bedroom's bathroom, he discovered that his cherished companions had scratched each other and his pillow thoroughly, and those brave warriors were lying on it in utter exhaustion. The professor, being far more concerned with their well-being than that of the furniture, tried to make them as comfortable as possible by sleeping in a chair, then took them the next morning to a veterinarian who wrapped them in bandages; after which their appearance resembled that of tied slabs in a deli display.

This interchange should not have been surprising; even one *without* them knows, cats and dogs are often foes, at least according to popular opinion. Of course, there are many heartwarming examples of these creatures living in peace, even in cooperation. But this ideal was not made manifest in these particular characters. Rather than learning that prejudice is a two-edged sword and giving it up out of their mutual affection for the professor, the only knowledge they gained from this whole sorry incident was that of their equal strength, which resulted in a kind of on-and-off armistice. But again, we will consider its character later.

As indicated, their pompousness persisted, and that night, the professor was met by the upsetting sight of two hairy lumps engulfing his pillow again. Regardless of their sentiments toward each other, both wanted the pillow, and both had proven capable of fighting for it, so tolerance was unavoidable. His remorse for their wounds moved him to give it up that night also and then the next, and the next, and so on. Then came the day when their bandages were removed.

That night, the professor resolved to repossess the cushion. And upon seeing that the former invalids had taken it again, he attempted to assert his authority. At first, he softly petitioned them to move while gently poking their sides. This method accomplished little besides relieving the dog of gas after one regrettable poke at his intestines.

After a minute of coughing violently with watery eyes on account of said gas, the professor took a deep breath, after stepping outside of his bedroom, and tried a firmer strategy. Standing over his pets in such a way as to cast a shadow over them, the professor pointed at the stubborn blobs and then gestured to the foot of the bed, all while making his point in as commanding a voice as he could muster when talking to such beloved company. This proved less effective than poking. So he used another "hands-on" approach. Risking another attack of flatulence, he took hold of the dog's side with both hands and pushed, evoking only a groan of annoyance. The professor then resorted to shoving, which, with its great girth, was no small feat. But this was certainly more stimulating, as the dog curled its upper lip to reveal a set of formidable teeth that seemed most unfitting compared to its body of jelly, and this curious mismatch was matched by a low growl from behind them. Though he specialized in records of human behavior, the professor perceived these reactions to be those of a peeved pet, and so redirected his attention to the cat, who was quicker to demonstrate its defiance by opening its mouth fully to release a hiss followed by aggressive gurgling. And all this was accompanied by long claws, which the cat used to threaten the would-be usurper and anchor itself to the fabric.

Never before had the professor felt so betrayed. His was a mixture of anger, sadness, and fear. But of this trio, sadness proved the strongest; unwilling to take further measures, he returned to the chair and tried to make himself as comfortable as possible. The one advantage of these failures was that the professor got to sleep sooner than the previous nights. Depression is a powerful sedative.

Of course, the professor's intellect did not stop at history. And he did not take this kind of treatment lying down. This point was literal for several more nights, but during this time, he landed one victory—the reclamation of the pillow. The solution was fairly simple: Wait for the animals to get up for the day, then snatch and hide it until night came. Then the professor used it to support his head and back, all the while under the burning glare of his beastly burdens. To regain his bed fully, eventually, the professor also revoked his pets' passes into the bedroom altogether, a punishment for which both blamed the other absolutely; but being a man of mercy, he furnished them with replacements.

CHAPTER 2

Though their bluffs were intimidating, neither the dog nor the cat injured any part of the professor, excepting his heart, of course. But this cannot be said for their own interactions. Both were convinced of the supposed superiority of their respective kinds, and their lavish lifestyles only strengthened those prejudices. They delighted in trying to justify them by making each other look weak and foolish. They never again engaged in direct conflict but instead developed all sorts of schemes to irritate, aggravate, and subtly torture. One fine example was the dog's "drool pool" plan. When certain that its adversary was absent, the dog would lazily stroll to the cat's water bowl, then after a couple head twists to be doubly sure of its solitude, it would stretch its head over the bowl, hang its jaw loose, let its tongue out, and dangle this appendage until the drink was thoroughly tainted. Then the dog would meander away, all the while snickering at its slyness.

When the cat discovered this pollution, though not before having a few laps, revenge was imminent. Its plan was more complex and, if successful, would prove all the more cruel. When a fresh bag of litter had been poured, it went to the box, gingerly crawled inside, and like the dog, made a last-second scope. Then the cat laid in it and rolled to and fro on its back, filling its fur with the coarse grains. Then it got out and almost walked on air toward the dog's bed, trying to drop as little evidence as possible. Another look around, and then the cat got in and repeated its rolling. Satisfied with this seasoning, the cat hopped out and went about its day, eagerly awaiting the canine's self-assumed bedtime. Needless to say, sleep did not come easy to the poor pooch, and with each arrival, it brought dreams of pins and needles.

This could not continue; the tricks and traps became so common that the pets were on the verge of nervous breakdowns. So they came to an agreement, not a treaty, but rather a contract more in keeping with their pettiness. As the proverb says, "The one walking with the wise will become wise," and by observing the professor practice his lectures, eavesdropping on his phone calls, or watching his choice of TV programs, these animals gained insight into academia, including one of its most revered institutions, a true mark of the civilized world: public debates. The pets watched with awe as some of society's most powerful and respected figures offered controversial theories, overturned established reasonings, and employed such eloquent language when sharing insults as to make them sound like compliments. Surely, this was a much better manner of elevating one's stature than through violence, if for no other reason than being much less hazardous to the health of the opponents.

It was settled—they would hold a formal discussion, one befitting the most prestigious college or capital and attended by spectators from far and wide. But debates alone would not be enough. After all, what good would it be to sway a crowd in one's favor, only to resume the same standard of living afterward? Such glory lacked staying power, lacked purpose. Theirs would be one of consequence; theirs would be a trial. Of these witty and hallowed gatherings, none seemed greater than that of a trial. Its air of officialdom was almost overwhelming. To come before a judge, a sage, to watch the robe ebb and flow with every step, to hear the knocking of the gavel, to see that one sit on a high bench and thus be closer to heaven, to consider that one considering the parties as a god, and to be rewarded with solidarity, while the enemy is condemned to a state worse than death.

This was the answer they were looking for! The arrangements were as follows: The trial would be held in the backyard. Since their rescue, the dog and the cat held the outdoor world in contempt, regarding it all as something raw and disgusting that should be reserved for "savages," but they believed that such an occasion as this would attract a crowd, especially those of the unwashed masses. If the professor were present at the proceedings, he was not likely to welcome any guests into the house from the "wild" side of the neighborhood, and even in his absence, the dog and cat reasoned, this innumerable audience would leave more than a few traces of their filth wherever they were, so the outdoors was the safest choice. Besides, this "vulgar" setting was hardly an untamed wilderness, as the professor was very fond of flowers and fresh vegetables, and thus had been maintaining a miniature Eden since before their adoptions, with the garden types beside each other, and these were shaded for some part of the day by a large pecan tree on the opposite side of the yard. From this cradle of nature's fragrant locks, they would beckon a figure of reverie to the privilege of honoring their sacred arguments with the fruitage of divine deliberation. And according to this verdict, the party found to be the greatest would remain with the professor, while the loser would be sentenced to a sudden disappearance, leaving all personal property without so much as a tearful goodbye. Of course, neither party intended to keep this malediction should they be found lacking.

7

CHAPTER 3

After crafting their arguments, the pets made a procession to the court, like brave warriors to the battlefield, but before a struggle of wit and rhetoric, came one with the pet door. The dog was the first through it, that is, only his first part got through. Though he squeezed and strained, it was to no avail. The issue was due, not only to a bloated belly, but also to the saggy condition of his skin, the folds of which compiled as they dragged against the frame, until they made a skirt of flesh around his rear. Had he stayed there and continued to pull for the rest of the day, this small exercise may have shrunk him to a more compatible size. The cat, however, did not have the patience, and so she provided another solution to this blockage, namely, a swift claw in the rump. This proved to be as effective as it was simple, producing what was likely the only instance of a flying dog without the aid of wings or balloons. The cat had a much easier time getting through, partly because she was smaller, but also because of the many hours of grooming that had slickened her fur and removed tangles.

While licking his wounds, the dog intensely eyed the fiendish feline. He wanted to bite off her tail, as he thought one pain in the butt deserved another. But before this was attempted, the dog remembered his surroundings, that there may be witnesses to the deed and that one of these may be the prospective judge. So the dog deigned to restrain his anger and took comfort in the certainty of the cat's expulsion after the sentencing. As he slowly got up, took a deep breath, and continued toward the garden, the cat was surprised at his exhibition of self-control but quickly decided to tempt it further, turning her head back as she passed just enough for the dog to see the corner of her mouth turned in a smirk, a gesture to which the dog revealed his tongue.

Taking their seats on patches of pansies, as they thought their posteriors too good for the ground, the would-be orators began to beckon all who chose to come and marvel at this matching of minds. They cried louder and longer than they ever had before. A large attendance was required, as they believed the reputations of their entire respective species was at stake, and this would be the definitive discourse by which the winner's kind would be vindicated for all time as humanity's perfect companion. Being as they were unused to such vocal exertions, it was only after several minutes that the dog and cat were heaving and panting; the dog was, in fact, in fear of passing out. When they had recovered, the opponents looked all around to welcome a myriad of admirers. Instead, they found the backyard almost as empty as before.

There was nobody in the pecan tree, nobody on the fences, and nobody on the ground, aside from the now-embarrassed rivals. They looked at each other and then toward the house, but before they could start back, a harsh cough-like sound came from above.

They discovered its source to be a raven that had seated itself atop the tall rosebush in one of the back corners. Examining this bird, it seemed to them the most wretched creature they had ever seen: It had a large scratch in one eye, which, combined with the odd tilt of its head to give the other one greater focus, suggested that the one scratched was rendered useless. Its wings were tattered, only two tail feathers remained, and one of its legs was missing a foot. Though its blackness gave the raven an ambiance of dignity, naturally resembling that of a judge's wear or even a priest's stole, to the dog and cat, this was little compensation. The raven, for its part, thought itself to be as good of a judge as any. Though its appearance gave no such credit, the raven was thoroughly educated, having nested at many centers of civilization: courthouses, churches, city halls, etc.

The dog viewed the bird with some difficulty, as the folds of his forehead covered the upper halves of his eyes. The cat viewed it with particular disdain, thinking that she would not have even eaten such a disgusting vermin when she lived in poverty, let alone regard its opinions as anything, and much less now. So she got up and started toward the house. There were petals stuck to her butt, and she shook some off with every step. But when she was halfway to the house, she heard the low gargling voice of the dog, and turning back, she saw that he had gotten closer to the raven and now sat on a stand of daisies.

CHAPTER 4

His address to the amateur mediator was as follows:

> "Before the beginning of man, there were canines, and as man established himself, he saw in the wolf a unique potential, which was to result in the greatest partnership of man and beast that the world has ever known. From Mesopotamia to Egypt, to China, to India, to North-, Meso-, and South America, and everywhere in between, we, as the descendants of those rustics, have helped man not only survive, but also thrive. In the wilderness, dogs have helped man get food. On the farm, we have helped man protect food. And in the city, much like man, we have reached the pinnacle of our greatest: risking our lives to destroy plague-ridden pests, capture dangerous criminals, and even rescue victims of every kind of disaster, from fire to hurricanes. And not only do we perform such daring feats as these, but when the dust settles and the smoke clears, dogs are there to help those suffering to heal and the disabled to function. From protecting food supplies to preserving cleanliness, certainly, no cat has proven so capable as we in every facet of society."

The dog ended with a sharp turn of his head toward the cat, which made his jowls and ears swing, adding to the dramatic flair.

By now, the discerning reader will wonder how any animal could have such a rich knowledge of its heritage. In this case, the dog, just like the cat, got such material from the professor's TV programs or, else, from his books, not because they could read but, rather, because the professor had the habit of reading aloud.

The cat's whiskers twitched with rage. She was not going to let him call her incapable before anyone, even a dumb, decrepit, oversized crow. She too approached "the bench" but walked until she was between the dog and raven. Before speaking, she raised her rear toward the dog and stretched her arms toward the raven, making sure to also display claws; this seemed a perfect way to insult one party and threaten another simultaneously. Her expression was nothing if not aloof, and she carried her speech with the most casual of tones:

11

"As my opponent has noted, his kind is common, and though they may be jacks of all trades, they are masters of none, especially when it comes to the hunt. While in flight or a nest, you have likely witnessed many dogs as they helplessly barked at birds and squirrels sitting on ledges or branches far beyond their snouts as their lack of agility is pathetic. Perhaps you have been among such quarries. Regardless, no doubt you know that cats are not so limited, and in fact, your own wounds may be evidence of our prowess."

This last statement was accompanied by a small smug grin. One may rightly expect the raven to have been shocked or outraged by such a direct and personal insult, but his face and resolve were concrete. He had suffered things far worse than snide remarks, and seeing that this was to be a mental duel between creatures that would usually try to eat him, he had prepared himself for the worst. So long as they did not physically assault him or each other, and the insults were kept at a minimum, he would give them an opportunity for defense and an impartial verdict.

The cat continued:

"As for companionship, cats are the most affectionate of all creatures. Anyone small enough can lay on a lap, but we, possessing natural massage skills, do as much to relax our caretakers as they do for us. We are also the gentlest of animals as can be seen by our treatment of legs. Dogs practically jump up them and risk pushing their owners over, while cats caress calves with our cheeks. Finally, during his petty world tour, my opponent failed to mention the high regard which my kind was given in Egypt, that its gods were made in our image. Thousands of years later, such cults continue, as the Internet is littered with our pictures and videos, and these may garner so much attention as to make us equal to human celebrities, if not more so."

13

CHAPTER 5

Having made her own case, the cat turned to sneer at the dog; after which, both watched the raven. They waited and waited and waited; he did not move, he did not blink, as if frozen in time. "Oh, forget it;" cried the dog; "the old bird is either sleeping or dead! *I* am going back in!"

But just as he was about to rise, the "old bird" spoke or, rather, croaked. "Let each one examine what he alone is doing and be proud of himself alone and not compare himself with others. For each one will carry his own load."

The parties looked at the raven and then at each other and again toward the raven, and there was one word on their tongues: "What?"

The raven continued:

"I heard those words from a church once. I had built my nest on a windowsill. Churches tend to have big colorful windows. It means that if I am to judge you, it must be according to your own deeds. Neither those of your ancestors nor others of your species. So then may both of you boast of what you yourselves have done, and by these accounts, I will judge you."

Now the parties were frozen. Again, they looked at the raven then at each other and again at the raven; this they repeated several times, but neither said a word. The raven, seeing that this odd game would go on indefinitely without intervention, looked intensely toward the dog, since he was the first to give a witness, and questioned him directly, "Concerning all the heroic acts of which you have spoken, which of these have you accomplished? Have you brought down the beasts of the woods for your master's table? Or defended his house from burglars? Or pulled him from a blaze? Speak up! Speak up! So that I may judge you. If you have only done so much as bring him a paper, by this I will judge you, but you must speak."

His face looked dumbfounded, and if not for its fur, one would see it bare a blush of embarrassment. He turned again to the cat, who also wore a kind of confusion. Silent, the dog stared at the ground.

"Come now, dog," said the raven. "Here you have spoken of lands and times far beyond our own, but do you have nothing to say for yourself? Even if yours is only that of an exterminator, this too is a blessing to your master. Tell me, how many pests have you killed or, else, driven away?" The raven pointed the damaged wing at the vegetable garden. "Surely a garden so lush and beautiful as that must draw many intruders," he surmised.

The dog became angry at the examiner's persistence. "Am I the only one being tried?" he shouted before lifting a paw toward the cat. "Why do you not ask her such questions? Did she not claim to be an expert at these things, with a greater body for such work?! Put the question to her!"

"I would not dare foul my mouth with vermin!" she protested, having lost her casualness. "Besides, such a revolting career is unnecessary." She then walked to the border of the two gardens and pulled part of a berry bush to reveal a cage trap. "Though this may seem strange to your type," the cat sneered toward the raven, "we, in the civilized parts of the world, let technology do the dirty work for us, which allows us all the more time to play and relax, and while I am not so big on playing, my caretaker and I always help each other relax. Many times I have laid on his lap, gently kneaded it like a ball of dough, and settled. And when he has petted me, I have rewarded him by the soft sound and shake of my purring, which eased him to slumber."

Snort

The cat looked toward the grinning dog. "What?" asked she, irritated.

"Oh, do not mind me," said the dog. "I was only thinking of all the times you have ignored the old man when he called you to his lap and, of course, that time when he picked you up and set you on his lap direc—"

"In case you have forgotten, dog," growled the cat, "you had your chance to speak. So if you do not have anything to say for yourself, then you have no business saying anything about me!"

"What happened next, dog?" asked the raven.

"What?!" shouted the cat.

"I want to know what happened," said the raven.

"Well, it is none of your business either, so stay out of it!"

"If I am to pass an honest judgement . . .," the raven started.

"Who are you to judge me?!" spat the cat. "I do not care about what anyone else thinks, especially not a stupid, trashy old thing like you!"

"Well then," said the dog, "you should not care what the raven thinks about this."

"I told you to be quiet!" shouted the cat.

The dog furrowed his many eyebrows. "I will say what I want to say," said the dog, his voice dripping with malignant ego, "and if you have a problem with that, my teeth are ready." Here he tried to brandish the aforementioned weapons, but they were mostly hidden by curtains of jowls.

The cat had no trouble showing her claws again. Her blood was boiling, but she did not want to risk any of it being spilled. She well remembered the shape she was in last time, and that was only for a pillow; her bandages had itched constantly. She also understood that her condition was not apt for direct combat. The same was true of the dog, but his larger size made him more intimidating. So the cat only seethed silently as the truth became known.

"As I was saying," said the dog, "the old man took hold of her, with great difficulty I might add, and carried her to his chair. Then he sat and set the cat on his lap. As soon as she was on her feet, she tried to jump down, but her 'beloved caretaker' took her into his arms. And so she reacted as any friend would by shredding his arms! So bad were the cuts that he spent the rest of the afternoon at the doctor!"

"I have the will and the right to do whatever I want, whenever I want," hissed the cat. "And at that time, I did not want to be on his lap! He would not take no for an answer, so I had to resort to violence!"

The dog turned his face toward her; he would have turned entirely, but the face alone was much easier. "You always hurt him," the dog continued. "Even when you are not trying! Many days he has started with pants covering his legs, only for them to be replaced by bandages, thanks to your so-called 'massages.' 'Kneading his lap like a ball of dough'—HA! What kind of a baker kneads with knives?! And all this would be bad enough if it was unavoidable, but you refuse to let him ease the pain by clipping those needles, even scratching him when he tries!"

The cat's whiskers were twitching so fast they could scramble eggs, and the slits of her eyes narrowed. Then she closed them and took a deep breath. "Well," she said, "at least I am not disgusting!"

"Disgusting?!" gasped the dog.

"Yes, dis-gust-ing!" the cat fired. "Inside and out! There is no other beast with as sour a smell as a dog! And as if that were not enough, your kind also sicken their mouths and stomachs by their own excrement!"

It was at this point that the armistice was nearly broken; though they stood in place, vibrations were visible in their viscosity. Their speech became unintelligible, degraded to senseless growls and hissing. But above this obscenity, there was another hideous racket, somewhere between a bellow and a whistle.

"CAAAW!!!"

It shook these fighting fools to their bones. The excitement was so great that for a second, the cat became cross-eyed. Both of them shook their heads and rubbed their ears. Then slowly looked up to the source of the monstrous scream.

18

CHAPTER 6

"There will be order in the court," said the raven, his voice now a little hoarse, as he had not called so strongly for some time. "As of yet," he continued, "both of you have only succeeded in exposing all the reasons why the other party should go, but neither of you have explained why you should stay." The raven then focused on the cat. "You have explained how you help your master, ahem, I mean, 'caretaker,' sleep. But while 'a handful of rest is better than two handfuls of work, a sluggish person will go hungry' or, rather, 'they should go hungry,' that is what I have heard, but I see that you eat very well despite doing little work, if any." Here the raven slowed his pace. "Could it be that it is your caretaker who is starving?"

"You are more ignorant than I thought," snarled the cat. "Our caretaker does not lack for anything, especially food."

The raven then looked at the dog.

"For a fact, you do not know what you are talking about," the dog affirmed. "Not only is his table always filled, but the old man also always has the most delicious things to eat."

The raven may have wondered how the dog knew these meals were so tasty; that is, if the answer could not be easily found in his shape. Another pause, but with a low bubbling hum from the raven, when they finished baking, his thoughts were related in an illustration:

> A man planted two fruit trees, both a different tree. He also dug pits around them, and these he would constantly fill, and the man said, "Surely they will produce fruit, and I will take pleasure in them."

> But he gave them too much water, and many roots rotted. Also, the trees became diseased, and when they produced fruit, all of it was rotten, so that the trees became waste, both of them. The man ate the fruit and became sick, so sick that he would vomit, but he continued to water the trees and to eat from them, even though he knew them to be the cause of his illness, and his hunger was never satisfied, but he continued to be ill and to vomit, for he kept saying to himself: "One day, they will produce fine fruit." He persisted until he starved.

"So it has become with you and your master. He took you in and gave you everything you wanted, even more than you wanted, and you have become rotten, both of you." He emphasized their sameness by waving his good wing between them. "He is starving himself of affection because he continues to put up with you, and you neglect or even refuse to return his kindness, if not on your own terms. He has brought this on himself, but you have only added to his pain because you choose to be useless burdens."

Again, there was silence. The dog and the cat stood absolutely still. Now they heard nothing besides ringing, their eyes were fixed on the raven. Even the dog's gaze, in spite of his forehead folds, was strongly on him so that the rest of the world was but a blur. Then the cat's tail slowly switched back and forth, and the dog's lips slowly parted, showing grit teeth.

CHAPTER 7

Then suddenly—

"REEEE - OOOOW!"

"BARKBARKBARKBARK!"

They exploded forward in a vitriolic flood. The raven, as noted earlier, had expected something like this, but even he was surprised by their sudden charge. The cat, despite her weight, was faster than the dog, though whether this was because of natural ability or the dog being in worse condition is uncertain. Whatever the cause, she reached the bush before he did. The raven jumped in flight and just in time. The cat pounced so strongly as to pass the top of the bush, perhaps the fuel of hatred gave her such strength, and swiped for the raven while both were in midair. Her middle claw caught one of his tail feathers, and the raven cried as it was plucked. But the cat would soon feel much more pain. "Pride is before a crash," and so it was that after falling, she landed in the midst of the thorny bush. It took her a moment to realize what had happened, but upon perceiving the green spikes piercing her pelt, the cat burst from this flowery torture chamber with a blood-curdling "REEEOOOW!"

Also, "a haughty spirit (is) before stumbling," so it was with the dog. While making his way to the bush, he tripped on a rag of skin and so tumbled the rest of the way, coming to rest at its feet or, rather, roots. Lying on his back, the dog saw the raven fly toward the house, over the house, and disappear behind it. He growled after it but was interrupted by the sound of suffering and was confused to find it coming from the bush. Then he saw the cat escape toward the sky; her figure got smaller and smaller and larger and larger. She was now falling, and her fall was heading toward him. The dog began rolling back and forth in a panic, trying to right himself. Perhaps it was best he fell, for though the impact was quite painful and pressed out all his breath, their combined corpulence cushioned them from serious harm, and the cat bounced off him.

For some time, the cat writhed in pain; while the dog gasped and coughed, partly because of the collision, but also because he had done more that day than he had since becoming one of the professor's charges. The same could be said for the cat, but the dog's larger size made him especially exhausted. In time, they were able to get back on their feet, first the cat and then the dog a little later. As she watched the dog lay in pain and tiredness, the cat wondered why she did not feel happy; likewise, when the dog got up, he thought he would like to kill the cat for such an attack, even though it was really an accident, for once, but instead, he just felt *sad*. The cat and the dog looked at each other then toward the bush, then toward the roof, then toward the pet door, and finally back at each other. They made their slow walk back to the door, heads hung, the cat ahead of the dog. But the cat stopped, and as the dog passed her, he saw that she seemed to have found something. Stopping, he looked toward the house and then the cat again. Since he was still out, the dog decided to satisfy curiosity.

Reaching her, he saw that she was standing over a black feather. For a moment, he was confused, as he did not observe the cat remove it from the raven because of his fleshy blinders, but soon determined its original owner. They continued staring at it, the remnant of a sage. Then the cat walked over it, squatted, relieved herself, and carried on. The dog watched as she passed then returned his focus to the now wet feather. Then he turned, raised his leg, and soaked it further; then also kept going. There were very few things the cat and dog agreed on, but one was this: that raven proved more stupid than they had expected, and though this may seem impossible, from then on, they hated that whole avian race more than each other.

24

CHAPTER 8

The target of their ire kept flying until he reached one of the town grocers. There, he saw a food truck in the parking lot and that some of his smaller cousins, the crows, were pecking at whatever the diners dropped. So he joined them. Upon seeing him, the crows took his conversation, and after the strange events of that evening had been related, one in the audience asked with a full mouth, "So"—here she paused to swallow—"do you think those pomps will ever stop fighting?"

The raven looked at her then at the crumbs clinging to her beak, then toward heaven. "I do not know," said he, "but probably not." The raven pecked another morsel, swallowed it, and added, "They are too much like people."

Eventually, he was satisfied and bid his relatives farewell, but before taking flight, the raven noticed a cacophony of creaking and rattling. And its sound seemed to be getting closer. A turn of the head revealed the source: a shopping cart, a very old and rusty shopping cart, rolling down the sidewalk. It was filled with bags of what themselves sounded like cans and bottles. The one pushing the cart looked almost as sorry as it did, his jacket was but a jumble of thread with jagged fringes, and his pants were worse. The hair of the head and face were his only substantial covering. But what interested the raven most was his partner—a dog, a dog with thin, greasy, weather-beaten hair; the leash of which was tied to the man's arm. Its belly was thin enough that in the absence of hair, one might see the outline of its organs. The man and dog seemed to walk especially slow, even considering their load, and the reason for this became apparent when they reached the point where the walk ramp met the lot's entry way. Just before they crossed this threshold, a car swung in; disaster seemed immediate. But then—

"ARUUUUW!!!"

Hearing the howl, the man stopped shy of the car's path. It also alerted the driver, who panicked and slammed his brakes in mid-turn, so that the side going into the turn was lifted off the ground for a couple seconds as it spun. When the car settled, all was silent; the raven, the crows, and all the human onlookers kept switching their gaze between the car and the man. The man looked on from the sidewalk, still clutching the basket, but his eyes and head floated back and forth, as if he did not know what to look at or, rather, what there was to look at. A short time later, the driver got out and focused squarely on the man.

"Hey, BUM!" the driver shouted. "What's wrong with you?! Get out of the road! You see this car?! You have any idea how much this cost me?! Enough to *buy* you! And you better hope you didn't dent it with that bucket of trash, or I'll be denting *you*!"

The driver then ran to the side of the car that had faced the man and frantically inspected it. The man stood there for a moment more, reaching down and fumbling his hand in the air until he touched the dog and rubbed its head; the dog, in turn, licked the hand. The man then gave a little smile, and both went on their way. When the driver heard the rattling of the cart, the driver turned and shouted, "Why don't you go jump in a lake?! If you don't *drown*, then at least you'll get a *bath*!"

The man just kept walking.

"Hmph," the driver scoffed and muttered, "stuck-up trash." Then the driver got back in the car and went to find a parking space.

The raven, for his part, watched the car roll by then turned to watch the man pushing his cart and the dog keeping perfect pace beside him. His focus, again, was primarily on the dog. Aside from the obvious malnutrition, it was healthy. Why then did it choose to rely on someone who could barely rely on himself to prevent injury to its master and, thus, make itself vulnerable to injury? Surely the leash did not always stay tied to the man's arm. Probably, it could get away without the man's notice, survive on its own, beholden to no one other than itself; maybe even find a new master, one who was more capable. But still it chose to stay. Why??? Why would anyone make such sacrifices? If not for food, if not for security, then for what???

"Love."

"What?" asked one of the crows.

"Hmm?" asked the raven.

"You said *love*."

"Oh . . . oh, never mind. On second thought, maybe the cat and dog are not so much like people," said the raven, "but some people are like them." With that, the raven took a jump, flapped his wings, and flew away.

29

Printed in the United States
by Baker & Taylor Publisher Services